THIS CANDLEWICK BOOK BELONGS TO:

For all at the special care Baby Unit,
RMH, Belfast

First U.S. paperback edition 1994.
First published in Great Britain in 1993 by Walker Books Ltd., London.
Library of Congress Cataloging-in-Publication Data
Jeram, Anita.
The most obedient dog in the world / Anita Jeram.—
1st U.S. pbk. ed.
Summary: Neither rain nor sleet nor curious passersby can move a very patient dog
who has been told by his owner to wait, but then a cat comes along.
ISBN 1-56402-264-1
[1. Dogs—Fiction.]   I. Title.   PZ7.J467Mo   1994   [E]—dc20   92-43768

10 9 8 7 6 5 4 3 2

Printed in Hong Kong
The pictures in this book were done in pen and ink and watercolor.

Candlewick Press,
2067 Massachusetts Avenue,
Cambridge, Massachusetts 02140

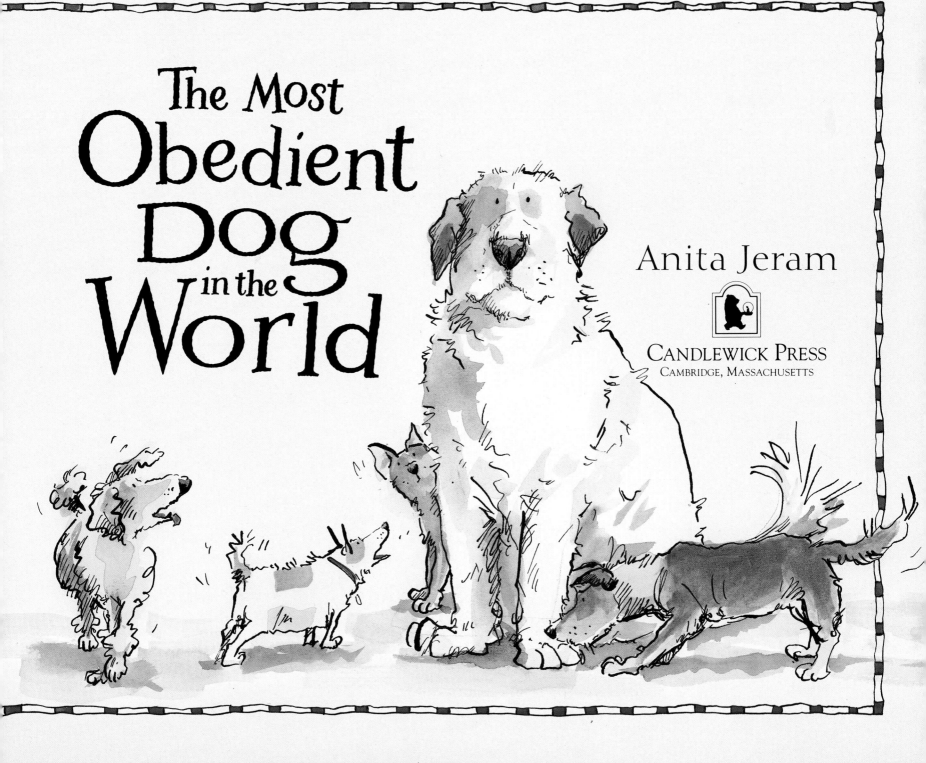

The Most
Obedient
Dog
in the
World

Anita Jeram

CANDLEWICK PRESS

CAMBRIDGE, MASSACHUSETTS

The most obedient dog in the world was
waiting for something to happen

when Harry came up the path.

"Hello, boy," said Harry.

The most obedient dog in the world wagged his tail and started to follow Harry.

"No . . . sit!" said Harry. "I won't be long."
And then he was gone.

"Why are you sitting there?"
asked a nosy bird.

"Are you going to sit
there all day?"

The most obedient dog in the
world didn't answer.

He just sat and waited
for Harry.

Big, fat raindrops began to fall.

"I'm leaving," said the bird. And he flew away.

Everyone ran for cover, except
the most obedient dog
in the world.

Thunder rumbled, lightning flashed,
and then the hailstones fell—

lots and lots of hailstones!

When the sun came out again
the bird flew back. The most
obedient dog in the world
was still sitting there
waiting for Harry.

"What a strange dog," people said as they passed.

Other dogs came
to take a look.
They sniffed and
nuzzled and nudged
and nipped,

but they soon got bored
and went away.

The most obedient dog in the world sat . . .

and sat . . . and sat . . . and sat.

How long must he wait for Harry?

Just then, a cat came by.

"Quick!" said the bird, pulling his tail.
"Why don't you chase it?"

The dog's eyes
followed the cat.
His nose started
to twitch,

and his legs started to itch.
He couldn't sit still
any longer.

He sprang to his feet . . .

and saw Harry!

"Good boy!" said Harry. "You waited!
Leave that cat. Let's go to the beach!"

The dog looked at the cat, and he looked at Harry.

Then he went to the beach with Harry.

After all, he was . . .

the most obedient dog in the world!

ANITA JERAM has illustrated several books for children, including
All Pigs Are Beautiful by Dick King-Smith, also published by Candlewick Press.
She is married to a paleontologist and has one son.